Patrolman Pete

A Day at the Seaside

AA Published by AA Publishing.

This book belongs to

© Automobile Association
Developments Limited 2006

AA Publishing is a trading name of
Automobile Association Developments Limited,
Fanum House, Basing View, Basingstoke, Hampshire RG21 4EA.
Registered number 1878835

A CIP catalogue record for this book is available from The British Library

ISBN 0-7495-4899-1
978-0-7495-4899-5
A02982

Printed and bound in China.

A Day at the Seaside

Written by Michelle Hogg

Molly and Tom were really excited. It was a lovely hot day and they were going to the seaside. Molly was wearing her favourite sun hat and Tom held a brightly coloured beach ball on his lap.

"Daddy, are we nearly there yet?" they cried from the back seat of the car.

"You'll be able to see the sea once we've gone over this hill," their daddy replied.

Suddenly, the car went CLUNK! BANG! HISS!
It got slower and slower until it stopped.

"Oh, no," cried the children. "What's happened?"

Tom and Molly's daddy turned the key, but the car wouldn't start. He opened the bonnet and looked at the engine, but he didn't know how to fix it.

"This is a job for Patrolman Pete!" he said. "I'll phone Rita at the call centre."

Rita asked for directions to the broken down car. "Don't worry," she said. "Pete will be with you in just a few minutes."

Meanwhile, Patrolman Pete, Stan the Van and Trevor the Toolbox were getting ready for another busy day.

"Phewee, Trevor, it's hot today, isn't it?" said Pete. "On a nice day like this, we should be at the beach!"

"Oh, yes!" said Trevor. "I'd love an ice cream!" Then he grinned. He'd just remembered one of his jokes. "Hey, Pete! What's a ghost's favourite food?"

"I don't know, Trevor. What is a ghost's favourite food?" said Pete.

"I-scream!" Trevor chuckled.

Pete had to laugh, just because the joke was so bad!

Stan came over to find out what all the noise was about. "Hey, you two, what's so funny?" he asked.

Pete told Stan the joke. "Oh dear, that's terrible!" cried Stan.

At that moment, Pete received a call from Rita.

"Hello, Pete," said Rita. "A family needs your help. They are on their way to the seaside, but their car has broken down."

"Righto, Rita!" Pete replied. "We're ready to roll!"

It wasn't long before Pete, Stan and Trevor reached the broken down car.

"Hello, Pete!" cried Molly and Tom. "Do you think you'll be able to fix our car?" they asked. "We want to go to the seaside!"

"I'll do my best," Pete replied.

"That's great, Pete," said the children's mummy and daddy. "Come along, children. Let's go to the park while Pete fixes the car."

With the children playing safely away from the road, Pete looked under the bonnet.

"Pass me the spanner, please," Pete said to Trevor.

"Here it is," Trevor replied from Pete's side. Trevor loved helping Pete. He always made sure that the tools they used were in top condition at the start of every day.

"Hmmm," said Pete, leaning over the engine. "I'll try the hammer next, please."

"Ready when you are!" said Trevor, holding the hammer up to Pete.

"It's no good, Trevor," said Pete with a sigh. "The engine is so badly broken that it needs to be fixed at a garage. I'll ask Rita to send along Rosie the Relay Truck."

Pete told the family the bad news.

"Oh, dear," said the children's daddy. "We won't be able to visit the seaside today."

Molly and Tom were very upset. They had been looking forward to paddling in the sea.

"Isn't there anything we can do?" Stan asked Pete.

"Don't worry," said Pete. "I've got an idea." He whispered his plan to Stan.

Stan grinned. "What a good idea," he whispered back. "The children will be really surprised!"

Rosie the Relay Truck beeped her horn as she came up the hill. The children ran up to the fence to watch.

"Hello, Rosie," said Pete. "We need your help. This car needs to be taken to a garage to be fixed."

"No problem!" said Rosie. "Stand back while I lift it onto my trailer."

Pete made sure that the car was safe, then he called to the family, "Climb aboard, everybody – it's time to go!"

Once the family had fastened their seatbelts, Rosie beeped her horn again. "We're ready to roll!" she called to Stan.

"Follow me to the garage, Rosie," said Stan.

"Is it far?" asked Rosie.

"You'll soon see," said Stan. It was time for Stan to put Pete's plan into action. He turned on his flashing lights, checked for traffic, then led Rosie onto the road.

As Rosie followed Stan over the hill, Molly pointed through the window and shouted, "Look over there! Look, Tom, look!"

"It's the sea!" cried Tom.

"We're going to the seaside after all!" they shouted together. "Hooray!"

Pete's plan had worked. By giving Stan directions to a garage on the seafront, the family could spend a day at the beach while their car was being fixed.

Pete and Trevor helped Rosie unload the car, while Molly and Tom went to buy ice creams with their mummy and daddy.

"I want to buy an ice cream for Patrolman Pete," said Molly.

"And I'll buy one for Trevor," said Tom.

The children carefully carried the ice creams back to the garage.

"Thank you for bringing us to the seaside today," they said.

"We're glad we could help," said Pete with a smile.

Pete and Trevor ate their ice creams, while the children played on the beach at last.

"I didn't really think we'd come to the seaside today," said Trevor.

"Nor did I," said Pete. "I wonder where we'll be going next."

Suddenly the radio crackled. "Hello, Pete," said Rita. "I have a job for you. A car has broken down on the way to the airport."

"Righto, Rita!" Pete replied. "We're ready to roll!"

Collect all of the Patrolman Pete adventures!